How Are They Made?
T-shirts

Wendy Blaxland

Marshall Cavendish
Benchmark
New York

This edition first published in 2009 in the United States of America by Marshall Cavendish Benchmark.

Marshall Cavendish Benchmark
99 White Plains Road
Tarrytown, NY 10591
www.marshallcavendish.us

First published in 2008 by
Macmillan Education Australia Pty Ltd
15–19 Claremont Street, South Yarra 3141

Visit our website at www.macmillan.com.au or go directly to www.macmillanlibrary.com.au

Associated companies and representatives throughout the world.

Copyright © Wendy Blaxland 2008

Library of Congress Cataloging-in-Publication Data

Blaxland, Wendy.
    T-shirts / Wendy Blaxland.
        p. cm. -- (How are they made?)
    Includes index.
    ISBN 978-0-7614-3812-0
    1. T-shirts--Juvenile literature. I. Title.
    TT675.B43 2008
    391--dc22
                        2008026213

Edited by Anna Fern
Cover design, text design, and page layout by Cristina Neri, Canary Graphic Design
Photo research by Legend Images
Map by Damien Demaj, DEMAP; modified by Cristina Neri, Canary Graphic Design

Printed in the United States

Acknowledgments
The author would like to thank the following people for their expert advice: Nick Barclay, Organic Cotton Advantage, Australia; Doug George, University of Queensland, Australia; Armelle Gruère, statistician, International Cotton Advisory Committee; Heidi Mitchell-Bradshaw and Sharon Scott, Bonds Australia; Guy Roth, Cotton Research Council, CSIRO, Narrabri; John Stanley, School of Environmental and Rural Science, University of New England; and Brooke Summers, Cotton Australia.

The author and the publisher are grateful to the following for permission to reproduce copyright material:

Front cover photograph: Red tshirt © stocksnapper/iStockphoto; green tshirt © Clayton Hansen/iStockphoto;. Images repeated throughout title.

Photos courtesy of:
© adidas, **24**, **25** (right); © Marronex/Dreamstime.com, **5** (top); © Photojay/Dreamstime.com, **5** (bottom left); © Studio/Dreamstime.com, **11**; Adrian Bradshaw/Getty Images, **17**; China Photos/Getty Images, **19**, **26** (left); Hola Images/Getty Images, **23**; John Kobal Foundation/Hulton Archive/Getty Images, **7**; Fred Mayer/Getty Images, **28** (left); David Dow/NBAE via Getty Images, **20** (bottom); Chris Hondros/Newsmakers/Getty Images, **9**; Stella/Getty Images, **4** (center); Stockbyte/Getty Images, **30** (bottom); Serge Attal/Time Life Pictures/Getty Images, **21**; Eliot Elisofon/Time & Life Pictures/Getty Images, **6**; © Michael Blackwell/iStockphoto, **14**; Philips, **10** (bottom); Photos.com, **4** (right); © Tara Todras-Whitehill/REUTERS/PICTURE MEDIA, **18** (left), **22** (bottom); © terekhov igor/Shutterstock, **8** (bottom); © Ginae McDonald/Shutterstock, **16** (bottom); © Sherry Yates Sowell/Shutterstock, **4** (left); Your Mantras, www.yourmantras.com.au, **27** (bottom), **29** (right).

Headshot illustrations accompanying textboxes throughout title © Russell Tate/iStockphoto

1 3 5 6 4 2

Contents

Glossary Words

When a word is printed in **bold**, you can look up its meaning in the Glossary on page 31.

From Raw Materials to Products

Everything we use is made from raw materials from Earth. These are called natural resources. People take natural resources and make them into useful products.

T-shirts

T-shirts are soft tops made in a "T" shape, usually with short sleeves. T-shirts are pulled on over the head. They generally do not have buttons, pockets, or collars.

The main raw material used to make T-shirts is cotton. Cotton fabric is made from the fluffy fibers that surround the seeds of the cotton plant. T-shirts can also be made from **synthetic fabrics**, such as polyester. Polyester is made from **petrochemicals**.

The T-shirt fabric can be colored with dyes and decorated with printing inks. Inks and dyes are usually made from synthetic chemicals.

The fluffy fibers from the cotton plant, called cotton bolls, are made into fabric for T-shirts.

YOUR AD HERE

Why Do We Need T-shirts?

T-shirts are cheap, comfortable clothes that keep us covered and warm. Everyone from babies to senior citizens wears them.

A T-shirt can make you a human billboard. Many people express their personalities through T-shirts, with printed slogans and pictures that show their fashion sense or promote events and products.

T-shirts are very popular in most cultures, so making them is big business.

T-shirts may be specially printed for a group.

St. Patrick Catholic School
SHAMROCKS

Reverent
Trustworthy   Responsible   Respectful
Caring of Others   Honest
Pledge
to be

When one wearer outgrows a T-shirt, it is often handed down to a smaller wearer.

The History of T-shirts

Guess What!

T-shirts began both in the United States and England as sailors' underwear. It was not until the 1950s that they were worn as outer clothing. Now, everyone wears them.

Many countries, particularly Britain and the United States, built their wealth on cotton and the clothing trade in the 1700s and 1800s. This wealth was created by the hard work of African-American slaves in the United States and the workers in the British colony of India who worked on the cotton plantations. The workers were often treated very badly.

T-shirts through the Ages

300 BCE
Cotton cloth is first brought to Europe, but it is expensive.

5000 BCE
Evidence of cotton cloth from this time has been found in Mexican caves.

1500s
Cotton cloth is made in France.

800s CE
Cotton cloth is made in Spain.

Mid-1800s
Cotton from the southern United States grown by African-American slaves makes white planters rich.

4000 BCE
Cotton is grown in India, then **exported**.

Late 1700s
Cloth made of Indian cotton becomes Britain's main export.

5000 BCE   2500 BCE   1 CE   500   1500   1800

In World War II, U.S. troops wore T-shirts.

LIFE
AIR CORPS
NEVADA
GUNNERY SCHOOL

After the actor James Dean wore a T-shirt as outerwear in the film *Rebel without a Cause*, so many people copied him that doing so changed from daring and rebellious to respectable.

Question & Answer

Where does the word T-shirt come from?

This is unclear, but many people refer to the shape of the shirt as a "T." The T might also refer to the army using T-shirts for training.

1914–1918
In World War I, Europeans use lightweight undershirts. The U.S. Navy copies them in cotton.

1932
A sweat-absorbing shirt is developed for a U.S. university football team.

1920s
T-shirt is first included in a dictionary.

1939–1945
In World War II, the U.S. Navy and Army issue T-shirts as standard underwear.

1950s Actors Marlon Brando and James Dean wear T-shirts without shirts over them in films.

1959 The invention of plastisol, a more durable and stretchable ink, allows more variety in T-shirt design.

1960s T-shirts are used for advertising and protest. A cotton and polyester blended fabric, which needs less ironing, is developed for T-shirts.

1970s Colored T-shirts become popular. Iron-on and realistic photo **transfers** are developed.

Late 1990s
Information, materials for sale, and services are available through the Internet, allowing people to print or buy T-shirts with their own designs.

1900

1925

1950

1975

2000

7

What Are T-shirts Made From?

Most T-shirts are made from cotton fabric. They may also be made from cotton mixed with synthetic fibers, such as polyester, to prevent wrinkling, or stretchy **elastane** to help them cling. Some T-shirts are even made from hemp or bamboo fibers.

Colored T-shirts are dyed, mostly with chemical dyes. They can be printed with plastic- or water-based inks, generally made from petrochemicals. They may also be decorated with embroidery, sequins, and many other materials.

The label on a T-shirt often shows the size, material, the place where it was **manufactured**, and washing instructions.

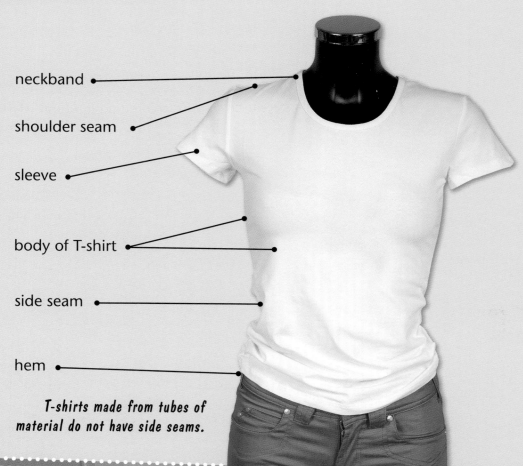

neckband

shoulder seam

sleeve

body of T-shirt

side seam

hem

T-shirts made from tubes of material do not have side seams.

Materials

Many different materials are used to make T-shirts. As with the making of all products, energy is also used to run the machines that help grow the cotton, mine the oil for synthetic fabrics, weave or knit the cloth, produce the dyes, and make and decorate the T-shirts.

Materials Used to Make T-shirts

Material	Purpose and Qualities
Cotton	Used to make cloth, thread, and some labels. Cotton fabric is soft, warm, **flexible**, long-lasting, **absorbent**, allergy-free material that breathes well.
Polyester	Used to make cloth, thread, and labels. Polyester fabric is wrinkle-free, strong, and long-lasting.
Elastane	Elastane can be used in cloth to add stretchiness.
Tape	Fabric tape sewn over seams makes them stronger and prevents them from ripping.
Elastic	Flexible elastic in the neckline of a T-shirt lets it stretch to prevent seams ripping, and keeps it sitting neatly.
Dyes	Dyes are used to color the cloth and thread.
Inks	Inks are used to print colored designs and slogans onto the body of the T-shirt.

Slogans on T-shirts can inspire both the people who wear the T-shirts and those who read them.

T-shirt Design

Specially trained designers create T-shirt designs for manufacturers. They decide which material to use. It might be cotton grown in a **conventional** way or **organically grown**, polyester and other synthetics, a mixture of cotton and synthetics, or even fabric made from hemp or bamboo.

T-shirt designers also need to decide:

✳ how heavy and stretchy the fabric will be

✳ whether the fabric will be woven or knitted

✳ the type of neckline

✳ the length of the sleeves and body

✳ whether it will be plain or decorated

✳ if and how it should be printed.

New technology, such as fabric glow with computer-generated light, is used in some T-shirts.

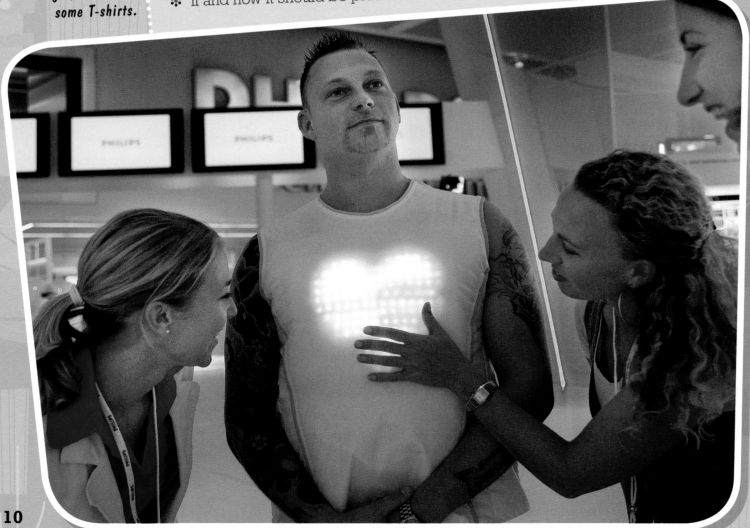

What Does a T-shirt Say About the Wearer?

T-shirts reflect the culture and fashion of the time. In the 1960s, tie-dyed T-shirts demonstrated the fashion for individual, colorful clothing. Some T-shirts advertise products. Others make a political or social point, or show a person's favorite TV show or his or her sense of humor.

In the 1980s, some T-shirts used special dyes that changed color when heated. Now "lumalive" T-shirts show bright moving pictures or words on flexible cloth panels powered by a tiny computer which is removed for washing. Some T-shirts with video screens and speakers can even play movie trailers. Other T-shirts can receive text messages from cell phones and one T-shirt can actually give you a hug!

Guess What!

Some T-shirts are free. However, the most expensive T-shirt ever was auctioned for $42,000. The money went to underprivileged children. It was the last in a series of limited-edition T-shirts auctioned by T-shirt manufacturer Hanes as part of its sponsorship of the 1996 Olympic Games.

11

From Cotton to T-shirts

The process of making everyday objects such as T-shirts from raw materials involves many steps. In the first stage, the cotton is harvested and the fiber separated from the cotton seed. The fiber is then sent to a spinning mill to be spun into yarn, which is knitted into stretchy T-shirt cloth. In the second stage, the T-shirt material is cut into pattern pieces, which are then sewn together. During the final stage, the T-shirt is printed or decorated and has a label sewn onto it.

Stage Two:

Stage One: Making Materials for T-shirts

First, the cotton is grown and harvested.

Next, the cotton fiber is cleaned and separated from the cotton seed in a **gin**.

Then, the cotton fiber is sent to a spinning mill. There, it is combed into long strands and spun into cotton thread.

The cotton is then bleached white or dyed different colors.

Finally, the cotton thread is knitted into cloth.

Stage Three: Decorating T-shirts

First, the slogan, image, or other decoration for the T-shirt is designed.

⬇

Then, the design is printed on the T-shirt with inks and dyes.

⬇

Next, the T-shirt is heated, if needed, to permanently fix the design onto the fabric.

⬇

Other decorations, such as embroidery, are added.

⬇

Finally, labels are sewn onto the T-shirt, usually on the neck at the back.

Making T-shirts

The cloth is cut into pieces according to a pattern.

⬇

Then, the pieces are sewn together.

⬇

Finally, a neckband is sewn on.

Guess What!

Almost all cotton grown worldwide has been developed to be white, because it is easier to dye. However, some cotton plants produce different shades of brown, and there is even some green cotton. Several companies produce colored cotton for sale on a very small scale. There are also several companies that dye cotton with colored clays instead of chemicals.

Raw Materials for T-shirts

The major raw material for T-shirts is cotton, the world's most widely used natural-fiber cloth. Cotton is soft, easy to dye, absorbent, breathable, and comfortable. It is warm in winter and cool in summer.

Cotton grows in one hundred countries in tropical and semitropical areas. Growing cotton needs a lot of water, and this has caused problems in some places.

Question & Answer

Was cotton first used in India or in South America?

Both! People discovered how to use different varieties of cotton thousands of years ago independently in both India and South America.

This cotton crop is being watered by a giant sprinkler system.

ARCTIC OCEAN

NORTH AMERICA

✪👕❖ United States of America

ATLANTIC OCEAN

PACIFIC OCEAN

✪ Brazil

SOUTH AMERICA

ANTARCTIC OCEAN

Centers for T-shirt Production

Most of the world's T-shirts are made in China, which uses 40 percent of the world's raw cotton in a range of clothing. So, while China does grow cotton, it also buys cotton for making T-shirts from some of the many other countries growing it. The United States grows cotton and makes T-shirts, too. However, it sells most of its cotton to other countries, where it is cheaper to manufacture clothing like T-shirts.

Question & Answer

Which British town was nicknamed Cottonopolis in the 1700s?

Manchester, because it was the heart of the worldwide cotton trade, on which it depended.

Key

- ✪ Important cotton-growing countries
- 👕 Important T-shirt-manufacturing countries
- ✤ Important cotton-manufacturing countries

This map shows countries that are important to the production of T-shirts.

15

Stage One: Making Materials for T-shirts

The basic material for T-shirts is cotton fabric.

Growing the Cotton

Cotton needs water and lots of sunshine to grow well. In countries such as the United States, cotton farms are very large and use modern technology. In poorer countries, cotton farmers often have small farms and little access to the latest farming methods. Their lives can be very hard.

On modern farms, the fluffy cotton bolls are picked by machine and pressed into huge cubes, called modules, which are then taken by truck to the cotton factory. The raw cotton fiber is called lint. A machine called a gin cleans the leaves and sticks from the lint, and separates the lint from the cotton seed.

The lint is then pressed into **bales** and separated into different grades. Longer fibers make a higher grade of cotton. Next, the lint is taken to the spinning mill to be made into fabric.

The cotton bolls are picked and pressed into modules.

Question & Answer

How many people work producing cotton worldwide?

An estimated 350 million people work making cotton, either on farms or transporting, ginning, baling, or storing it.

At the spinning mill, cotton fiber is made into yarn.

Spinning the Yarn and Knitting the Fabric

At the spinning mill, the lint is sorted. Longer fibers make stronger thread or yarn. First, the fibers are cleaned. Then they are **carded** to separate them, and laid straight, ready to be put together into one long strand.

Several strands are combined to make a thin strand, or sliver. Then the slivers are twisted together to form the final yarn. Yarn can also be combed to produce extra fine or shiny cotton, or combined with polyester fiber for strength and to help prevent wrinkling.

The yarn may now be dyed different colors or bleached white. Then it is wound onto a holder called a bobbin, ready to be weaved into fabric.

Most T-shirts are made of knitted fabric that molds to the body. Big knitting machines knit the yarn into a series of **interlocking** loops. Much T-shirt fabric is made in tubes of the right size. Other knitting machines make smaller tubes of especially stretchy fabric for the neckbands.

Guess What!

Fabrics can be treated for special effects. Washing with bleach, sand, or stones softens and **distresses** fabrics. Washing with **enzymes** ages the fibers. Washing with silicone softens fabrics.

Stage Two: Making T-shirts

Making T-shirts is a fairly simple process, which is mostly done by machine in large factories. In some factories, workers use specially designed machines to cut, put together, and sew an entire T-shirt. Elsewhere, different workers each perform a separate part of the process, using specialized machines.

First, the pieces of cloth to make the T-shirt must be cut according to the pattern pieces. These differ, depending on the size and shape of the final T-shirt. Often, computers make sure that the least amount of fabric is wasted. Lasers may be used to cut the fabric.

Question & Answer

How many T-shirts can be made from one 500-pound (227-kilogram) bale of cotton?

You can make 1,200 T-shirts from one 500-pound (227-kilogram) bale of cotton.

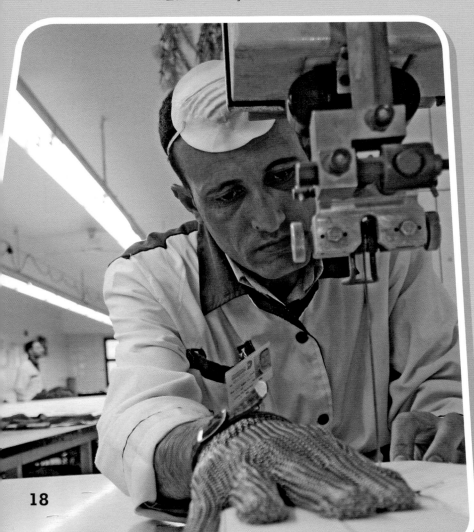

A worker uses a machine to cut out many pieces of cotton fabric at a time.

The fabric pieces are sewn together by machine.

Sewing

If tubed T-shirt fabric is used, the sleeves and body of the T-shirt do not need seams. If the fabric is not tubed, machines sew the front and back of the T-shirt together at the side seams.

The hems of sleeves are usually finished before the sleeves are fitted into the body of the T-shirt, since this is easier. Then the sleeves are joined on to the body with a seam.

Next, the shoulder seams are sewn, and a neckband is put on. The neckband and shoulder seams may be **reinforced** with tape or stretchy nylon. The neckband is then neatened by a row of stitching on top.

Guess What!

In one American factory, a team of workers, each doing a different part of the sewing process, turns out a T-shirt every eleven seconds.

Stage Three: Decorating T-shirts

Plain colored T-shirts before they are printed are called blanks. These blanks can be decorated by using dyes and inks. Some special inks puff up. Others glow in the dark, are glittery or metallic, or even change color when they heat up as you wear them!

There are several different methods of printing on T-shirts.

Screen Printing

Screen printing is a low-cost printing method. It makes a sharp-edged image by applying the inks directly to the T-shirt.

First, a stencil of the image to be printed is placed on a screen made of fine mesh. The stencil stops the ink from printing on the areas where it is not wanted. Ink is then pushed through the fine holes in the screen with a squeegee onto the T-shirt fabric.

Most T-shirt printing inks need to be cured or set by heat so that the ink will stay on the fabric. In most factories, this is done in special heating and drying machines.

This T-shirt has just been printed by a screen-printing machine.

Other Printing Methods

Designs from a computer can be directly printed onto polyester T-shirts using special dyes and an ink-jet printer. The dye is bonded permanently to the fabric by heat.

Other decorations may be sewn or embroidered onto the T-shirt, usually by machine, but sometimes by hand.

Finishing Touches

A label is generally sewn at the back of the neck opening with information about the manufacturer, fabric, size, and washing instructions.

The finished T-shirts are then inspected for accurate sewing, flat necklines, and clear printing.

These bundles of finished T-shirts are ready for packing.

Guess What!

Tightly woven, darker, and heavier T-shirts block out more of the Sun's harmful rays.

Packaging and Distribution

Products are packaged to protect them while they are being transported. Packaging also displays the maker's brand and makes products look attractive when they are sold.

The packaging depends on the type of T-shirt and where it will be sold. High-quality T-shirts may be pressed in steam tunnels before packaging. Some T-shirts are folded and packaged in clear plastic bags with product information on them. Others are folded around cardboard to keep their shape.

T-shirts for sale in stores often have hanging tags with extra information, such as price, which can be read by scanners.

Finally, T-shirts are boxed in dozens or half-dozens. Boxes may be shrink-wrapped with plastic to make bigger loads, which are then shipped in large, identical shipping containers.

Packing is the final stage of T-shirt manufacturing.

Question & Answer

What is the record for the most T-shirts worn by one person at the same time?

On an October 12, 2006, TV show, Matt McAllister donned a total of 121 T-shirts. They ranged in size from small to extra large.

Distribution

T-shirts are sold in a number of ways.

Many mass-produced T-shirts are sold to **wholesalers**, who buy large quantities. The wholesalers then sell the T-shirts to **retailers**, such as chain stores, department stores, and fashion stores.

T-shirts are often designed in one country, made cheaply elsewhere, especially in Asia, and then shipped back for sale in the original country. The actual T-shirts cost little, but everyone in the chain must add their costs and make a profit. Many retailers, however, are now buying directly from manufacturers rather than through wholesalers.

In contrast, some companies design and make their T-shirts in the one building, and even sell them through their own stores. These companies can quickly respond to what people want. Individual designers may also sell their T-shirts directly from market stalls.

Many T-shirt companies operate through the Internet. Customers design exactly what they want, send an electronic order, and the blank T-shirt is printed, packaged, and sent directly by mail.

T-shirts showing which country you support are an important part of attending international sporting competitions and show membership of a group.

Marketing and Advertising

Marketing and advertising are used to promote and sell products.

Marketing

T-shirts are fashion items and what sells changes rapidly. Customers include big companies, which give away T-shirts printed with advertising for their products. Groups, such as fans of particular bands, or people wanting souvenirs of a place or event, also buy T-shirts.

People may want T-shirts to show that they belong. On the other hand, they might prefer T-shirts with rare patterns and messages that show how individual they are. These sell for more, especially to T-shirt collectors.

T-shirt brands fight to keep customers loyal. They may stress qualities such as service or trendiness. T-shirt manufacturers also sponsor groups, such as bands, or big events to show what they value.

Guess What!

Fake T-shirts copy well-known brands. While some people feel they have been cheated, others think their copy is almost as good, and cheaper, too. Copying, however, really means stealing the designer's ideas and hard work.

This group of tennis stars, photographed at the 2004 Olympic Games in Athens, Greece, are wearing Adidas T-shirts because they are sponsored by the Adidas company.

ImPossible is Nothing

Australian swimming champion Ian Thorpe appears in advertisements for Adidas T-shirts.

Advertising

T-shirts are advertised both directly, through advertisements, and indirectly, when well-known or popular people wear them. Companies advertise in traditional media such as newspapers and magazines. T-shirts are included in general advertising handouts from chain and department stores, too.

On the Internet, new companies can have as big a presence as a major producer. Linking T-shirt websites to other websites helps promote them.

T-shirts are also advertising tools themselves, since their blank front and back make them an ideal and inviting billboard.

Production of T-shirts

Products are often made in factories in huge quantities. This is called mass production. They may also be made in small quantities by hand, by skilled craftspeople.

Mass Production

Most T-shirts are made by mass production. T-shirts can be made very cheaply in big numbers by complex machines in huge factories, generally in Asia. The quality, costs, and price are controlled and the same T-shirts are sold worldwide.

Custom-made T-shirts

Some people want to choose their T-shirt pattern or even design it themselves. Companies use online stores, which need a surprising number of workers, to help customers do this. Other companies let people first send in designs and then vote on them. Next, they make the most popular T-shirts. These T-shirts sell well to customers who buy not just a T-shirt but the story behind it.

Factories, such as this one in China, make huge numbers of T-shirts.

Small-scale Production

Individuals make or print T-shirts, too. It is fairly easy, cheap, creative, and satisfying.

Often, small-scale producers enjoy making T-shirts that reflect their beliefs. They may respect the environment and perhaps reject "big business" values. Some small manufacturers develop cotton with different natural colors, or dye T-shirts by stirring them in a bucket with clay.

These people can find marketing help online, where they can sell their T-shirts, too. There are even special chat rooms where people discuss how to make T-shirts.

People do not need much special equipment to silkscreen their own designs onto T-shirts.

T-shirts and the Environment

Making any product affects the environment. It also has an effect on the people who make the product. It is important to think about the impact of a product through its entire life cycle. This includes getting the raw materials, making the product, and disposing of it. Any problems need to be worked on so products can be made in the best ways available.

Growing Cotton

Most cotton is grown using large amounts of fertilizer, pesticides, and water. These methods produce as much cotton as possible. The chemicals, however, can affect workers growing the cotton. They may also pollute the water, soil, and air.

Growers in wealthier countries can use new cotton varieties with built-in pesticides to reduce the need for spraying. They also take care to recycle water. Organic cotton growers, however, do not like to use any chemicals at all.

Working Conditions

Working conditions in T-shirt factories vary widely. Some factories are not always safe or do not always pay fair wages. Workers can suffer lung damage from fibers in the air and other health problems. Nevertheless, conditions in many T-shirt factories are improving due to campaigns for fairer wages and better working conditions.

Spraying pesticides helps cotton crops to grow, but can cause problems in other parts of the environment.

Many people prefer to buy T-shirts made from organically grown cotton.

"I am my own guardian angel."

Recycling

T-shirts are perfect to recycle. Half the discarded T-shirts from the United States are resold abroad. The rest are sent to secondhand or thrift shops, made into rags, or shredded.

Cotton fibers break down because they are plant fibers and can eventually enrich the soil. Polyester can be recycled. Fleece T-shirts can be made from recycled **P.E.T. bottles**, saving energy compared to making new polyester.

Guess What!

T-shirts often travel around the world in their lifetime. They might be made from cotton grown in Europe, made into T-shirts in China, sold new in the United States and then sold again secondhand in Africa.

Questions to Think About

We need to conserve the raw materials used to produce even ordinary objects such as T-shirts. Making items from **renewable resources**, conserving water and energy, and preventing pollution as much as possible means there will be enough resources in the future and a cleaner environment.

These are some questions you might like to think about:

✳ What are the advantages of cotton T-shirts? Synthetic T-shirts?

✳ What will be the next trend in T-shirts?

✳ How can growing cotton and making T-shirts be made safer?

✳ What are the advantages and disadvantages of using organic cotton in T-shirts?

✳ What can you find out about T-shirts made from other fabrics, such as hemp and bamboo?

✳ What are your favorite T-shirts? Why?

Do you have a favorite T-shirt?

Glossary

absorbent
able to take in water

bales
large, tightly-packed bundles

carded
brushed to untangle the fibers before they are spun

conventional
in the usual way

distresses
makes a fabric look used

elastane
a fiber that can stretch five times its length without breaking

enzymes
substances that speed up chemical processes

exported
sent abroad to be sold

flexible
able to bend

gin
a machine that removes the cotton seeds from the lint

interlocking
looping together

manufactured
made, usually in a factory

organically grown
grown without the use of artificial fertilizers or pesticides

P.E.T. bottles
bottles made from a type of plastic called polyethylene terephtlalate

petrochemicals
chemical made from petroleum oil products

reinforced
made stronger

renewable resources
resources that can be easily grown or made again

retailers
stores that sell products to individual customers

synthetic fabrics
fabrics made by humans, often using petrochemicals

transfers
printed designs that can be transferred onto T-shirts

wholesalers
businesses that buy very large quantities of goods and sell them to stores, rather than directly to the consumer

Index